TROLLS,
Go Home!

First published in Great Britain by Bloomsbury Publishing Plc
Published in the United States by Bloomsbury U.S.A. Children's Books
175 Fifth Avenue, New York, NY 10010
Distributed to the trade by Holtzbrinck Publishers

Library of Congress Cataloging-in-Publication Data
MacDonald, Alan.
Trolls, go home! / by Alan MacDonald ;
illustrations by Mark Beech. — 1st U.S. ed.
p.   cm.
Summary: When the Trolls move next door to the Priddles, both families
find the other strange, which causes many misunderstandings.
ISBN-13: 978-1-59990-077-3 • ISBN-10: 1-59990-077-7 (hardcover)
ISBN-13: 978-1-59990-078-0 • ISBN-10: 1-59990-078-5 (paperback)
[1. Trolls—Fiction. 2. Neighbors—Fiction. 3. Individuality—Fiction.]
I. Beech, Mark, ill. II. Title.
PZ7.M145Tr 2007   [Fic]—dc22   2006049887

First U.S. Edition 2007
Typeset by Polly Napper/Lobster Design
Printed in the U.S.A. by Quebecor World Fairfield
2 4 6 8 10 9 7 5 3 1 (hardcover)
2 4 6 8 10 9 7 5 3 1 (paperback)

TROLLS, Go Home!

Alan MacDonald

Illustrations by Mark Beech

BLOOMSBURY
CHILDREN'S
BOOKS

MR. TROLL: Egbert / Eggy
Description : Tall, dark, and
searesome
Likes: Roaring, tromping,
hiding under bridges

MRS. TROLL: Nora
Description: Gorgeous (ask
Mr. Troll)
Likes: Huggles and kisses,
caves, the dark

ULRIK TROLL
Description: Big for his age
Likes: Smells, singing,
rockball

GOAT
Description: Strong-smelling,
beardy beast
Likes: Mountains, grass
Dislikes: Being eaten

PRIDDLES: Roger, Jackie, and Warren
Description: Pasty-faced peeples
Likes: Peace and quiet
Dislikes: Trolls

13⁵⁰

Tall, Dark, and Ugly

"**J**ACKIE! Come and see! They're moving in next door!"

Mr. Priddle had his telescope trained on a large, blue moving van parked in next door's driveway. His wife's voice floated up the stairs.

"Roger! I hope you're not snooping through that telescope."

"Of course I'm not," said Mr. Priddle, with his eye pressed to the telescope. "Wait! They're getting out! I can see . . . Good gravy!"

"What, dear?" Mrs. Priddle came into the front

bedroom holding two mugs of tea. She was followed by their freckle-faced son, Warren, who
had come upstairs to find out what all the fuss was
about.

"They're huge! Colossal!" exclaimed Mr. Priddle.

"Well, some people are tall," replied his wife.
"Just because you're a bit on the short side,
Roger."

"No, I mean *really* huge, Jackie. Take a look for
yourself."

Mrs. Priddle folded her arms. "I am not snooping on the neighbors through a telescope. What
will they think if they see you peering through
the curtains?"

"I don't mind snooping," offered Warren. "Let
me have a look!"

"In a minute, Warren," said Mr. Priddle, impatiently. "Good Lord! I've never seen anyone so
hairy!"

"Well, what if they are?" replied Mrs. Priddle.
"Just because you're bald as a newborn baby."

"I don't just mean *hairy*. I mean hairy *all over*,"
said Mr. Priddle.

"Now you're being ridiculous!"

"See for yourself!" said Mr. Priddle.

"Let me look! It's my turn!" cried Warren, making a grab for the telescope.

"Get your hands off, Warren!" snapped his dad.

"Don't be so childish, Roger," said Mrs. Priddle. "Let the boy have a look."

Warren pushed in front of his dad. Covering one eye, he used the other to squint through the lens. He could see one of the neighbors carrying a table toward the front door. The table was like the base of a tree trunk, but the creature—he couldn't really call it a person—carried it as if it was no heavier than a matchstick.

"Whoa! Ugly or *what?*" said Warren.

"Warren!" scolded his mother. "It's not nice to say that about people."

"But Mom, they *are* ugly," Warren pointed out.

"He's right, Jackie," agreed Mr. Priddle. "They're brutes. From what I've seen they belong in a zoo, not a house." He elbowed his son aside so that he could reapply himself to the telescope.

"You're making it all up," said Mrs. Priddle.

"We're not! Take a look for yourself!"

"I told you I am not spying on our neighbors

through a telescope. It's rude." Mrs. Priddle took a dainty sip of her tea.

"There's another one getting out," pointed Warren excitedly. "There are three of them!"

"Move over," said Mrs. Priddle. She smoothed back her blond curls and put her eye to the telescope.

"Oh, my giddy bananas," she said. "I don't feel well."

The Trolls moving into Number 10 would have been a surprising sight for anyone.

Mr. Troll was wearing a white undershirt, a baseball cap, and an enormous pair of bright red Bermuda shorts reaching to his knees. These were the only clothes he could find in the shop that were big enough to fit him. Mrs. Troll was wearing a flowery cotton dress jammed so tightly over her brawny body that any moment the buttons threatened to burst off and shoot in all directions. Only their young son, Ulrik, looked halfway normal. But it was difficult for any troll to look normal standing on Mountain View Street, Biddlesden, this sunny morning.

The Trolls had coarse brown hair sprouting all over their bodies. It hid their faces except for their coal-black eyes, their snoutish noses, and the two sharp white fangs that stuck out of either side of their mouths. Most trolls cannot be called beautiful. In fact, if you came upon a troll unexpectedly—say, by wandering into a deep, dark forest—you would probably scream and climb the nearest tree quicker than a startled squirrel. A troll's sheer size is enough to scare anyone. Their ugliness is legendary, enough to put a witch or a hag off her breakfast. Mr. Troll was roughly the size of a grizzly bear standing on its hind legs—and next to him Roger Priddle would have looked like a stick insect on a diet. Even their new house at Number 10 looked rather small, as Mr. Troll found out when he tried to get the table through the front door.

"Arghh! Gnnnh!" he roared. "It's too small."

"It can't be too small," said Mrs. Troll. "It's the same size as it always was."

"Not the table," groaned Mr. Troll. "The door! The door's too small for me to get in!"

"Well, use your head then," sighed Mrs. Troll.

Mr. Troll did. He thumped his big, hairy head against the door frame and the plaster above it caved in, leaving a space large enough for him to squeeze through with the table.

Next door, Mr. Priddle gasped. "Did you see that? He smashed the door to pieces! With his head!"

"I hope he's not going to do that every time he comes home," said Mrs. Priddle.

Inside Number 10, the Trolls looked around their new home. Sunny wallpaper brightened the walls and there were carpets on the floor.

Mr. Troll sniffed. "It's very clean," he grumbled.

"Don't worry, Egbert," said Mrs. Troll, "we'll soon change that. A nice bit of dirt on the floor, a few moldy leaves—it'll soon look like home."

"I like it as it is," said Ulrik. "Much better than our old cave."

Mr. and Mrs. Troll exchanged dark looks. Ulrik ran into the hall.

"Uggsome! There are stairs! Can I look up here, Mom?" he called, jumping them two at a time.

In the bathroom, the Trolls stared at the gleaming white bath.

"What is it, Mom?" asked Ulrik.

"It's a bath, my hairling," explained Mrs. Troll. "You lie down in it."

Ulrik climbed in and lay down. It was a tight fit, even for a young troll. His large, hairy feet stuck out beyond the end of the bath. "What's this?" he asked, twisting a silver tap around. The shower came on above, soaking him with a hundred tiny jets of water. "Ha ha! It's tickly!" Ulrik giggled. "I'm all wet!"

"Get out of there, Ulrik," growled Mr. Troll. "The rain's coming in."

"It's not rain, it's a shower," explained Mrs. Troll,

turning off the tap. "I read that peeples take a shower every day. To keep themselves clean."

"Clean?" said Mr. Troll, recoiling in horror. "You mean they wash? With water?"

"Yes, and something called soap."

"I want to wash with a soap!" shouted Ulrik.

Mr. and Mrs. Troll exchanged another worried glance.

"We don't want you smelling all sweet as a daisy," growled Mr. Troll. "Trolls smell of the forest, the earth, the dark. Those are the old Trollish smells."

Ulrik sniffed himself under his hairy arms. He liked his own smell. He wondered what peeples smelled like up close. Next time he got the chance he would make sure to smell one.

By dinner time, they were all hungry. It had been a long journey coming from the far, blue mountains of Norway. Mrs. Troll set a single can on the table in front of them. Mr. Troll pointed at it with his fork. "What's this?"

"It's called Baked Bean," said Mrs. Troll. "I got it at the shop on the corner."

Mr. Troll screwed up his nose in disgust. "Bean? I can't eat bean—what kind of a meal is that? Trolls eat meat! Where's the goat pie?"

Mrs. Troll sighed. "We're not at home now, Egbert. I don't think it's as easy to find goat."

"No goat pie?" Mr. Troll's mouth fell open.

"Don't blame me," said Mrs. Troll. "It was you who wanted to move here."

"We didn't have any choice, you know very well," said Mr. Troll, darkly. "How could we stay after what happened?"

"What did happen?" asked Ulrik, innocently. His parents had never explained why they'd left home in such a hurry. Mr. Troll covered his face with his hands.

"I don't want to talk about it."

"He'll have to know sometime," said Mrs. Troll.

"Know what?" demanded Ulrik.

"Ulrik," said Mrs. Troll, "your dad had a terrible experience. With a goat."

"No! Don't speak about it!" groaned Mr. Troll.

"He's got a right to know," insisted Mrs. Troll. "Are you going to tell him or shall I?"

Mr. Troll peered at his son over his hands. "It was a monster, Ulrik," he said. "A monster!"

"It was a billy goat, Egbert," said Mrs. Troll. "Don't exaggerate."

Mr. Troll looked at his son. "A giant goat, Ulrik. He had two brothers but next to him they were quite small. I faced him on the bridge. He had hooves like iron, hornses as sharp as knives."

"What happened, Dad?" asked Ulrik, wide-eyed. "Did you roar and chase him away?"

Mr. Troll shook his head, unable to speak the awful truth.

Mrs. Troll took over. "The goat charged," she said. "Your father lost his nerve and he got tossed from the bridge into the river. I had to drag him out by the ears, or he would have drowned."

"The shame of it," moaned Mr. Troll. "The shame!"

"So you see, Ulrik, that's why we had to move," continued Mrs. Troll. "Your father felt that if we stayed at home the other trolls would always be making fun of him."

"Beated by a goat! How could I look them in the eye again?" asked Mr. Troll, pitifully.

Ulrik went over to his dad and stroked his large, shaggy head. "Don't worry, Dad. I bet those other trolls would have run away."

"You think so?" Mr. Troll managed a smile.

"You faced a giant goat," said Ulrik. "I think you're the bravest dad in the whole world."

Mr. Troll gave his son a squeeze. He wiped away a speck of dirt that was making his eyes water. "What about this bean then, Ulrik? I'm starving," he said.

Opening the can was harder than Mrs. Troll had expected. She watched Ulrik trying to bite into it with his sharp teeth, but even a troll's teeth couldn't make much of an impression. Mrs. Troll tried cutting the can with her knife and fork, but each time it catapulted across the table like a slippery fish.

All this time, Mr. Troll's face was growing darker and darker. He was starting to growl—a sure sign that he was about to lose his temper. (Trolls have short tempers at the best of times, and Mr. Troll liked to boast he had the shortest temper of anyone he knew.) Finally he reached out and grabbed the can and flung it against the far wall with a great angry roar.

"GRARRR!"

The can burst open and a thick gloop of baked beans in tomato sauce began to slide down the wallpaper. Ulrik reached out a finger and dipped it in the sauce, licking it off with his tongue.

"Yum!" he said. "Baked bean is uggsome!"

But Mr. Troll had stormed out of the house, banging the door behind him.

Outside, the sight of the neat green lawn and the sickly sweet smell of the roses did nothing to improve his mood. All he could see for miles around were rows of identical houses. They had lawns and patios, wooden benches, and flowers in neat borders.

Biddlesden wasn't a bit like home.

He missed the lofty mountains of Norway with

their heads in the clouds. He missed the wide open skies, the shadowy pine forests, and the deep lakes that shone like mirrors.

The stars were coming out in the night sky. He looked for the North Star, turned his face in the direction of home, and sighed deeply.

A small, warm paw crept into his own and, looking down, he saw little Ulrik at his side.

"Don't worry, Dad," said Ulrik. "Maybe we'll have goat pie for dinner tomorrow."

"Humph," said Mr. Troll. "Let's go in. You can lick that bean juice off the wall."

As they went up the path, Ulrik thought he saw a curtain twitch in an upstairs room next door.

Roaring Lessons

ROGER Priddle liked Sunday mornings. What he liked best was lying in bed, knowing he didn't have to go to work at the bank. But on this Sunday morning his doze was disturbed by a deafening noise. It sounded as if a herd of wildebeest was stampeding through the house next door. Was it his imagination or was the room shaking? He looked up at the lamp hanging from the ceiling—it was definitely swaying to and fro.

He prodded his wife in the back. "Wake up, Jackie, I think it's an earthquake!"

"Huh? What?" said Mrs. Priddle.

"An earthquake! We're all going to die!"

"Don't be silly, Roger," his wife yawned, sleepily. "This is Biddlesden—we don't have earthquakes. Not on Sundays."

Then came the bellow from next door that made them both sit upright and clutch at the bedspread.

"What was that?" asked Mrs. Priddle. "It sounded like someone being murdered!"

"It's that family next door," said Mr. Priddle, grimly.

"Do something, Roger," urged his wife. "It's seven o'clock in the morning. Go over there and tell them to stop."

"Are you crazy?" asked Mr. Priddle. "Have you seen the size of them?"

"Well, we can't just lie here and listen to that racket."

The thumps and roars from next door were growing louder. Mrs. Priddle banged on the wall with her slipper. No one seemed to hear her.

At Number 10, Ulrik had woken up early. It was impossible to sleep when you were living in a new house where there were so many things to see.

He ran into his parents' room where he found them both asleep. Under their considerable weight the bed sagged in the middle like a hammock. Ulrik jumped on top of his dad's round belly, rising and falling in time with his snores, until Mr. Troll woke up.

"Come on, Dad!" said Ulrik. "Time for my roaring practice."

Mr. Troll groaned. "Isn't it a bit early?"

"You said I had to practice every day."

"All right, all right."

A few minutes later they were marching around the bedroom, stamping their feet as if they were crushing invisible ants. Sitting up in bed, Mrs. Troll watched her son proudly as he followed behind his dad, copying him.

"Remember," said Mr. Troll, "trolls don't walk. They tromp. They make the trees shake and the birdses twitter away."

"I like birdses, Dad."

"Are you tromping?"

"Yes, Dad," said Ulrik.

"Now imagine there is a goat just around the corner and you're going to scare it."

"Why do I want to scare it?"

"Because you're a troll. Trolls jump out and scare goatses. That's what we do."

"Couldn't I just say: 'Hello, I'm Ulrik!' "

"That's not going to scare anything."

"Or I could sing it a song. Mom says she likes my singing."

Mr. Troll rolled his eyes.

"Look, is this singing practice or roaring practice?"

"Roaring practice," admitted Ulrik.

"Then let's get on with it. Roar after me."

Mr. Troll gathered himself. He took a deep breath, swelled out his hairy chest, threw back his head, and let rip a roar like a thunderclap.

"GRAAARRR!"

This was the sound that made the Priddles sit bolt upright in bed, fearing that someone was being murdered.

"Now, you try," said Mr. Troll.

Ulrik gathered himself. He took a deep breath

and tried to swell out his chest like his dad. Catching sight of himself in the mirror, with his eyes screwed up and his cheeks puffed out, he thought he looked like a wrinkled old goblin. He fell back on the bed giggling. Mr. Troll patted his young son on the head.

"Don't worry. We'll have another practice tomorrow," he said.

As Ulrik ran off to play, Mr. Troll shook his head in despair.

"See what I mean? Harmless as a kitten."

"He's only young, hairling. Give him time," said Mrs. Troll. "I'm sure they'll have roaring lessons at school."

Later that morning, Mr. Priddle trained his telescope on next door's back garden. He had moved it into Warren's bedroom where he had a better view from the window.

"What are they doing now, Dad?" asked Warren.

"Shhh!" said Mr. Priddle. "He's just come out. The big one."

"He's a troll," said Warren unexpectedly.

"A what? How do you know?" asked his dad.

"I looked it up last night," said Warren proudly. "It's in my junior encyclopedia."

He showed his dad a picture of two large, snarling trolls—a male and female standing side by side. They weren't wearing Bermuda shorts or flowery summer dresses, but the resemblance was unmistakable. He read the caption below the picture.

"*Trolls: fierce race of creatures found in the mountains of Norway. They inhabit caves and underground dwellings.*"

"Good gravy!" said Mr. Priddle.

"But what are they doing here, Dad?" asked Warren.

Mr. Priddle shrugged. "I don't know. But he certainly looks mean. A brute. I wouldn't want to tackle him. With my judo skills I might get carried away and do him some serious damage."

Mr. Priddle had once taken up judo at an evening class. It seemed to involve wearing baggy, white pajamas and talking a lot about belts. Actually he had only attended one of the classes and had returned home grumbling that he'd been thrown around all night like a beach ball. Still, he liked to give the impression that he knew a thing or two about self-defense.

Mrs. Priddle came in and joined them by the window. Next door they could see Mr. Troll prowling around the garden. He appeared to be marking out a large area in the flower bed.

"What's he up to now? He's down on his hands and knees," said Mr. Priddle.

"Perhaps he's weeding," said Mrs. Priddle.

"No. He's . . . Good heavens! He's digging with his bare hands. Digging up the flowers!" said Mr. Priddle.

Showers of earth flew into the air behind Mr. Troll as he tore up the flower bed in much the same way as a dog digs up a bone.

"What's he digging for, Dad?" asked Warren.

"How should I know?" said Mr. Priddle. "Perhaps he wants to bury something."

"You mean like gold—or diamonds?" asked his wife, hopefully.

"Or a dead body," said Warren, in a low voice. They both looked at their son nervously and then back at the troll next door.

"It's certainly going to be a big hole," said Mr. Priddle. "He's going down deep."

"Maybe he's a murderer," said Warren. "Maybe they murder people and bury them in the garden."

Mrs. Priddle let out a faint scream. "They're living next door! It's not right, Roger. Why didn't they move in next to the Westcotts down the road? Why us? How do you expect me to sleep at night?"

"Now calm down, Jackie," said Mr. Priddle.

"I can't be calm. My nerves won't stand it, Roger. I want you to get rid of them."

Mr. Priddle put his arm around his wife. "Don't

you worry, sugarplum," he said. "I have a plan."

"Are you going to fight him, Dad?" asked Warren, hopefully. "Are you going to get him in a headlock?"

"No," said Mr. Priddle, drawing a red notebook from his pocket. "I'm going to keep a diary."

Teachers Are Weird

ULRIK stood in the garden looking at the hole his dad had dug in the flower bed. Where rosebushes had once bloomed, now there was only a tall mound of earth. Ulrik scrambled to the top and looked around. He caught sight of two eyes peering over the garden wall at him. They belonged to one of the neighbors—a plump, freckled boy with rosy cheeks. Ulrik waved to him and the two eyes promptly vanished from sight. He went over to the wall and found the boy crouched beneath it.

"Who are you hiding from?" he whispered.

Warren Priddle sprang to his feet in alarm and backed away. "Nothing . . . I . . . I think my mom's calling me," he stammered, making for the back door.

"Don't go," said Ulrik. "What's your name?"

"Warren," said Warren.

"I'm Ulrik."

"You're a troll," observed Warren. He was taking care not to get too close.

"Yes," nodded Ulrik. "And you're a peeples. Do you go to school?"

"Of course. Everyone goes to school," said Warren, scornfully. He decided the creature wasn't going to eat him after all.

"I'm starting school tomorrow," said Ulrik, proudly. "It's my first day. We could go together!"

Warren tried to imagine walking into the school playground with Ulrik. His friends would soon start avoiding him if he hung around with this hairy, ugly creature. He didn't want Ulrik telling everyone at school they were friends. For that matter, he wasn't sure he wanted a troll at his school at all. He would have to find a way to get rid of him.

"So. You've never been to school?" he asked.

"Never," said Ulrik. "Trolls don't have schools, but my dad's been teaching me. So far I've done roaring and tromping. Want to see?"

Ulrik tromped up and down the garden, stamping his feet and giving his best roar.

"Great," said Warren, when he'd finished.

"Is it?" said Ulrik. "My dad says my roar wouldn't scare a caterpillar."

"You should do that at school—all that roaring stuff," said Warren. "Mrs. Melly will love it."

"Who's Mrs. Melly?"

"Our teacher. We call her Mrs. Smelly."

"Mrs. Smelly," repeated Ulrik. He was a little confused. Perhaps teachers had two names.

"I suppose you've never met a teacher either?" asked Warren.

"Never," admitted Ulrik.

"Better be careful," Warren advised him. "Teachers can be weird."

"They can?"

"Yes. For instance, when you meet Mrs. Melly, she'll probably do this." He held out his hand to Ulrik. Ulrik looked at it, baffled.

"Why?"

"It's polite. That's how we say hello."

"Oh, I see!" said Ulrik. "And what do I do?"

Warren gave a weasel smile. "You bite it."

"Are you sure?" said Ulrik, doubtfully.

"Of course. Give it a good, hard bite or she'll think you're rude."

Ulrik shrugged. "Okay. Like this?" He took hold of Warren's pink hand and sunk his fangs into it.

"Arrrgh!" yelled Warren. "Let go!"

"Was that hard enough?" asked Ulrik.

Warren nursed his hand. His eyes were watering. "Perfect," he winced. "Do it like that and Mrs. Smelly will love it. She'll probably give you a gold star."

"Uggsome!" said Ulrik. "I've never had a gold star!"

Warren went back inside the house. His hand seemed to be bothering him. Ulrik was glad that he'd made a new friend. Not all peeples he'd met were friendly—some of them ran away just when you wanted to talk to them. But Warren seemed to like him and it was nice of him to explain about teachers' strange ideas. Ulrik couldn't wait to start school the next day. Wouldn't his parents be proud when he came home wearing a gold star?

A Nice Kid

THAT afternoon Mrs. Troll took Ulrik to the supermarket. She had tried asking for goat again in the local store, but they seemed to have only cans of the baked bean and something called spagotty hoops. She was pretty sure Mr. Troll wouldn't like it any better than the bean. He had been sulking a lot since they'd arrived in Biddlesden, and Mrs. Troll felt he needed some nice goat pie to cheer him up. She was sure the supermarket would sell goat, perhaps even a young kid, which was Egbert's favorite.

Ulrik had never been in a store like the supermarket. In fact this was only the second time he'd been in a store, so everything seemed new and exciting. It took some time before Mrs. Troll could drag him away from running in and out of the automatic doors. She let him push the cart with the squeaky wheels and he scooted up and

down, dodging in and out of startled shoppers who leaped out of his way.

"What are those, Mom? Can we try them? Please, Mom!" he begged. He was so excited that he forgot to look where he was going and crashed into the back of a young man in a blue jacket.

"Careful!" said the store clerk, turning to glare at him.

"Sorry," said Ulrik. He pointed at the cart. "I said 'Stop!' but it didn't listen."

Mrs. Troll came puffing up the aisle, out of breath.

"Ulrik! I told you not to go charging off on your own!"

"Sorry, Mom, but look! I found where they keep the meatses."

Ulrik pointed at the shelves on either side of the aisle, stacked with meat of every kind.

Mrs. Troll addressed the store clerk politely. "I was wondering, where do you keep the goat?"

"The what, ma'am?"

"The goat. Egbert likes goat pie, you see—it's his favorite—but so far I haven't been able to find it."

"We have turkey," said the clerk. He pointed to the rows and rows of meat. "Chicken, lamb, beef, pork . . ."

"No, it has to be goat."

The clerk scratched his head. No one had ever asked him for goat before.

"What about a kid?" suggested Mrs. Troll.

"A kid?" said the clerk.

"Yes, a nice, young kid. Tender, not too stringy. Egbert would love that."

A blond-haired woman, who was passing by with her cart at that moment, stifled a scream.

"I could roast it over a fire," said Mrs. Troll.

"Yum!" said Ulrik. "Roast kid!"

"I'm sorry," said the clerk. "We don't . . ."

But he didn't get any further. The blond-haired woman had fainted, passing out face down in her shopping cart so that it fell over with a huge crash.

"Roger, you won't believe it!" said Mrs. Priddle as soon as she burst through the kitchen door. "I've just heard the most terrible thing at the super-market."

"I'm just making some tea," said Mr. Priddle.

"I don't want tea. I want you to call the police. It's just as I thought, we're living next door to murderers. And worse than that . . ." She lowered her voice and shut the kitchen door. "They're *cannibals*," she hissed.

"Cannibals? Who? What are you talking about?" asked Roger.

"I just told you. I was in the supermarket, minding my own business, and there she was."

"Who, Jackie? Slow down!"

"Her—from next door! Who do you think?"

"Mrs. Troll, you mean?"

She looked at him in surprise. "How do you know her name?"

"Warren told me. It seems he's been chatting with the young one in the garden."

"Chatting? You let him *speak* to one of them? Are you out of your mind?"

"Don't worry, darling, he's fine. Just tell me what happened."

"Well, she—Mrs. Troll or whatever she calls herself—was talking to one of the store clerks. And I heard her say boldly: 'I want a nice, young *kid*. A kid to roast for dinner!' "

"A kid? What do you mean?"

"I mean a *kid*, Roger! A kid! Like our little Warren!"

"Good Lord! You can't be serious!"

"I heard her with my own ears. They cook them over a fire, Roger!"

Mr. Priddle gasped and sat down heavily on a chair. It was a nightmare. Their next-door neighbors were cannibals! Monsters! Child-eaters!

That would explain why the young one was so eager to "make friends" with Warren. He was lining up his next meal. Suddenly Mr. Priddle remembered something else.

"Jackie! He's going to Warren's school," he said.

"Who?"

"Ulrik. The young one. Warren says he starts school tomorrow."

Jackie let out a dramatic scream. She thought about fainting a second time, but her husband was the only one in the room and he wasn't much of an audience.

"We've got to do something," she said. "I'm calling the police." She picked up the phone but before she could dial, Mr. Priddle took the receiver from her and replaced it.

"Let's think about this, Jackie," he said. "If you tell the police now, they'll never believe you. Think how it will sound—cannibals living on Mountain View Street. They'll think you've lost your marbles. No, first we've got to gather evidence."

"How? I'm not sitting here waiting for them to eat somebody," said Mrs. Priddle. "They've probably had the paper boy already. What about my poor little Warren—going to school with that . . . that hairy savage?"

"Leave it to me," said Mr. Priddle. "I'm watching their every move. It's all in here."

He showed her the notes he'd made in his *Troll Watch Diary*.

"As soon as we've got enough evidence we call the police."

Troll at School

ULRIK gazed at himself in the bathroom mirror. He liked his new school uniform. True, the shirt was a bit on the small side. It only reached to his belly button and the pants looked more like shorts.

Nevertheless, he felt like he looked sharp. When he went downstairs his mother gave him a big huggle, lifting him right off the ground.

"Is this my little Ulrik?" she said. "All growned up!"

"Get off, Mom!" protested Ulrik, wiping away

the kiss she planted on his cheek.

"Now, don't forget," Mrs. Troll said. "Be good and do what your teacher tells you."

"I *know*, Mom," said Ulrik. "I've been talking to Warren. He's in the same class as me."

"That's nice, hairling," said Mrs. Troll. "I'm glad you're making friends already."

Later that morning, Ulrik met his class teacher and gave her his best smile. He thought she looked a bit surprised to see him. Her mouth was hanging open as if she was trying to catch passing flies.

The truth was, nobody had warned Mrs. Melly that "the new boy" was a troll. She had never met one before, though of course she had read about them in storybooks. She knew they were wild, fierce creatures who made a habit of hiding under bridges. This troll was bigger than she and was showing his two sharp teeth.

"You must be Ulrik," she said, a little nervously.

"Yes," said Ulrik. "And you're Mrs. Smelly."

The class dissolved into fits of giggles.

"Quiet!" barked the teacher. "My name is Mrs.

Melly, Ulrik, Mrs. Melly. Welcome to Class 4."

She held out her hand to him. Ulrik remembered what Warren had taught him. It seemed a strange way to greet a teacher, but then teachers were odd and he didn't want to be rude. He bit Mrs. Melly's hand as hard as he could.

"Yargh!" Mrs. Melly pulled her hand away and stared at the two fang marks imprinted on it.

"You bit me!" she said in astonishment.

"Did I do it right?" asked Ulrik.

Mrs. Melly had turned a deep shade of purple.

"At this school we do not *bite*," she said, icily.

"Oh. But Warren said . . ."

"You will sit down, Ulrik," said Mrs. Melly. "And if you *dare* to bite anyone again, I will send you straight to the principal."

Ulrik hung his head and slunk away to sit down. He had done exactly what Warren had told him, so why was his teacher so mad? He had so wanted to make a good impression on his first day and get a gold star. An idea came into his head. When he wanted to please his parents he showed them how his roaring practice was coming along. Warren had assured him that Mrs. Melly would love to see it. Maybe she wouldn't scowl so much when she saw how hard he'd been practicing.

Ulrik took a deep breath. He faced Mrs. Melly and tromped down the aisle, stamping his feet in the ant-crushing style his dad had taught him.

"*Graaarr!*" he roared. "*Graarrr!*"

Mrs. Melly was certain the troll was going to attack her. It was obviously working itself into a rage. She backed away until she was up against her desk, then she sat down on top of it.

"Now, stop that, Ulrik," she said.

"GRAAARRR!" roared Ulrik, making the windows rattle.

Mrs. Melly toppled over backward and disappeared from sight with a yelp.

Looking rather shaken, she emerged from underneath her desk and straightened her glasses. Ulrik looked pleased with himself.

"Uggsome! That was my best roar ever!" he said, beaming. But Mrs. Melly didn't seem pleased at all. She sent him to stand outside the principal's office. Mr. Wiseman sat him down and talked for a long time. He said that biting, stamping, and roaring was shocking behavior and he hoped Ulrik didn't behave like that at home. Ulrik answered truthfully that he did, but that only seemed to make matters worse. Finally he was sent back to the class.

Mrs. Melly sat him next to a girl named Nisha. Nisha moved her chair as far away from him as possible. None of the children sitting at the table spoke a single word to him all day. They all seemed to think he was going to try to bite them. Even Warren pretended not to notice when Ulrik waved at him across the class.

When the bell finally rang for the end of school, he was glad he could go home.

"Now," said Mrs. Melly, "don't forget—Wednesday is our trip to the farm. Ulrik, here is a letter to take home to your parents. And I expect you to be on your best behavior, is that clear?"

Ulrik nodded miserably. He was beginning to see why trolls didn't go to school.

The Sweet Stink of Home

WHILE Ulrik went to school, Mr. Troll got up late as usual. He came downstairs feeling as hungry as a very hungry horse. Since arriving in Biddlesden he'd had very little to eat. Trolls have enormous appetites and would look at an entire roast chicken as little more than a tasty snack. As Mr. Troll thumped downstairs, he thought he smelled the delicious aroma of goat coming from the kitchen. But it turned out he had imagined it. When he sat down, Mrs. Troll placed a can on the table.

He groaned. "Oh, no, not blunking bean again!"

"No," said Mrs. Troll. "This is different. It's called spagotty hoops."

Mr. Troll prodded the can glumly. "Do I have to throw it at the wall?"

Mrs. Troll shook her head. "I asked the lady in the store. She gave me one of these to open it." She held up a can opener with a sharp, hooked blade.

Mr. Troll yawned as his wife tried to work out what to do with the can opener. In the end, she raised it high in the air like a dagger and plunged it into the heart of the can. There was a puncturing "THWUCK!" Mrs. Troll wiped a squirt of tomato sauce from her eye and examined the hole she'd made. "Hmm," she said.

BANG! THWUCK! BANG! She attacked the can again and again until it had as many holes as a fishing net. "Pass me your bowl, Eggy," she said, panting for breath.

Mrs. Troll held the can over the bowl and some stringy globs of spaghetti hoops began to dribble into it.

"Ugh!" said Mr. Troll, peering at the bowl in disgust. "Looks like maggot soup."

He pushed back his chair and headed for the door.

"You haven't had any breakfast," said Mrs. Troll.

"I'd rather eat bat droppings," replied Mr. Troll, sulkily.

"Oh well, suit yourself," said Mrs. Troll. "You do the shopping if you're so picky."

She followed him into the hall. "Now where are you going?"

"Out," growled Mr. Troll shortly and slammed the door behind him.

Mr. Troll stomped off down Mountain View Street in the worst of moods. It's well known that trolls can be bad tempered in the mornings, but a troll who has started the day without breakfast in his belly is the kind of troll it's better to avoid. If there had been a thought bubble above Mr. Troll's head, it would have been filled with a big, black cloud.

As he reached the main road he headed into town without the slightest idea where he was going. Shoppers saw him coming and crossed to the other side of the road to avoid him. Most of them had never seen a fully grown troll before, and they certainly didn't expect to meet one stomping along High Street in Biddlesden on a gray Monday morning. Cars whizzed past like flies buzzing in his ear. Mr. Troll didn't like the noise or the smell they made. He longed to smell the sweet stink of another troll. Back home he might have run into one of his friends, Snorvik or Boglov, and he would have greeted him with a loud roar and a mighty huggle. But here the only creatures to be seen were pasty-faced peeples who flattened themselves against walls to let him go past.

He came to a set of steps leading down into a subway. It looked dark down there. Mr. Troll went down the steps hoping to find some kind of cave. The subway was dingy and deliciously smelly. A rumbling sound came from above him as cars passed overhead.

It reminded Mr. Troll of the old, wooden bridge back home where he used to hide and wait for the skinny goats to pass by. "Trip-trop, trip-trop," their little hooves would go on the bridge. How he enjoyed the moment when he sprang up like a jack-in-the-box to give them the fright of their lives. The look of surprise on their silly goat faces.

He closed his eyes, imagining he was back home again under the creaky, old bridge. He could hear footsteps descending the steps into the subway. Mr. Troll felt an urge to give something a thumping good fright. A roar was swelling up from deep inside him . . .

Meanwhile, back at home, Mrs. Troll was waiting for him to return. At first, she was angry with him. "Grouchy old grump-bag," she thought, "storming out like that just because he didn't like his breakfast."

Well, let him go hungry. What did he expect her to do, produce goats out of a hat?

But as the hours passed by she started to become anxious. She was used to Mr. Troll's sulks, but normally they didn't last longer than an hour or so. Yet when Ulrik returned from school there was still no sign of her husband.

Mrs. Troll stood at the window looking along the road anxiously.

"Hi, Mom," said Ulrik. "What are you doing? Where's Dad?"

"That's the trouble," replied Mrs. Troll. "He went tromping off down the road this morning and I haven't seen him since. Oh, Ulrik, I hope he's all right! He's never been far from the house before. What could have happened?"

Ulrik didn't know. He had wanted to tell his mom about his miserable day at school, but she seemed too worried to listen. He went and stood next to her, resting his head against her shoulder.

Just then a police car pulled up outside the house. A man and a woman in black uniforms got out. One of them opened the back door and out climbed Mr. Troll.

"Thank uggness!" said Mrs. Troll as she hurried to answer the door.

"Is this your husband, ma'am?" asked the policewoman.

"Eggy? I've been worried sick. Where have you been?" asked Mrs. Troll.

"I'm afraid he's been making a bit of a nuisance of himself," said the policeman. "We found him in a subway under High Street."

"Oh, Eggy!"

Mr. Troll looked down at his feet, embarrassed. "I just wanted somewhere to hide, somewhere

dark and stinksome. I only meant to fright them a bit, that's all."

The policeman looked at him. "You did that all right. Scared the living daylights out of them, jumping out and shouting like that."

"Roaring," corrected Mr. Troll. "I was roaring. *Grarrr!*"

"Don't start again," said the policewoman, sharply. "We had enough of that in the car."

"Are you going to prison, Dad?" asked Ulrik, tugging at his dad's arm.

"Not this time, son," replied the policeman.

"We'll let him off with a warning. But from now on he better behave himself. No more lurking in dark subways. No more scaring folks out of their wits. You nearly gave that old lady a heart attack!"

Mr. Troll remembered and smiled. "Her teeth jumped right out," he told Ulrik. "I never did that to a goat!"

"It's not something to be proud of," said the policewoman, sternly.

Mr. Troll tried to listen while the police talked for a long time about "not looking for trouble." He explained he hadn't been looking for trouble, he had been looking for a cave. But then the conversation got a little bit muddled. Finally Mrs. Troll saw the police out. But when she opened the front door there was someone else waiting outside: the neighbors from next door. It was turning into a strange day.

Mr. Priddle had seen the police car pull up outside the trolls' house through his telescope and had hurried next door with his wife.

"Are you arresting them?" he demanded hopefully.

"No, sir," said the policeman. "Just a misunderstanding—there's nothing to worry about."

"That's easy for you to say. You're not living next door to them," replied Mrs. Priddle.

"It's all in here, officer," said Mr. Priddle, brandishing his *Troll Watch Diary*. "All the evidence you need. Noise at all hours of the morning, biting people . . ."

"Biting?" said Mrs. Troll. "We've never bitten anyone!"

Ulrik hung back behind his mom and said nothing.

"Ask them," said Mr. Priddle, pointing. "Ask them why there's a great big pile of earth in their garden. Ask them what they're eating for dinner tonight!"

Mr. and Mrs. Troll looked at each other. "Bean," said Mr. Troll, gloomily. "It'll be that or maggot soup."

After much argument, the Priddles were eventually persuaded to return to their house.

"Don't worry, we'll keep an eye on them, ma'am," said the police officer.

"A big help that will be when we're all murdered in our beds," replied Mrs. Priddle.

"Why don't we all have a nice cup of tea to calm down?" suggested the policewoman.

"If somebody else mentions tea," said Mrs. Priddle, "I'm going to scream very loudly."

Next door the trolls sat around the table, sunk in gloom.

"Well!" said Mrs. Troll. "What was that all about?"

Mr. Troll propped his head in his hands. "It's no good," he said. "It's all my fault. We should never have come here."

"We've only been here a few days," Mrs. Troll pointed out.

"I miss the mountains," brooded Mr. Troll. "I miss our stinksome, old cave. I miss goat pie. I miss hiding under bridges and frighting goatses."

"It was you who wanted to leave home, Eggy," Mrs. Troll reminded him.

For a while they all sat in dismal silence.

"Ulrik, I completely forgot," said Mrs. Troll, suddenly. "How was your first day at school?"

"Oh . . . uggsome," said Ulrik, feebly.

"You see, Eggy," said Mrs. Troll. "Everything's going to work out fine. Ulrik's doing well at school and making lots of new friends, aren't you, hairling?"

"Yes," lied Ulrik. "Lots."

His mom and dad beamed at him fondly. How could he tell them the truth: that his first day at school had been a complete disaster? That he had no friends and no one spoke to him. His parents had enough to worry about already. Instead he took out Mrs. Melly's letter and gave it to his mom. Mrs. Troll read it through.

"A trip to a farm!" she said. "That sounds like fun!"

Goblins!

THAT night Mrs. Priddle couldn't sleep. She had been tossing and turning for hours. Every creak and groan of the house made her tremble like a leaf. At last she gave up and shook her husband by the shoulder. Mr. Priddle grunted and rolled over.

"Wake up, Roger!" said Mrs. Priddle.

"Eh? What's happening?"

"I can't sleep!"

Mr. Priddle groaned. "Whassamatter?" he

mumbled.

"I told you, I can't sleep. How can you lie there snoring like a pig when there are murderers living next door? What if I'm next, Roger? What if that brute comes for me in the night and snatches me away?"

"At least I would get some sleep," thought Mr. Priddle.

"What do you expect me to do, Jackie?" he asked. "You heard the police. They don't believe us."

"Then we'll have to *make* them believe us. We need proof, Roger. Proof that they . . . I can hardly say the word . . ." She lowered her voice to a whisper. "Proof that they *eat* children."

"What sort of proof?" Mr. Priddle asked. "I can hardly go next door and start poking around for evidence."

Mrs. Priddle fixed her husband with a steely look he knew all too well.

"No, Jackie," he said. "No, I can't . . ."

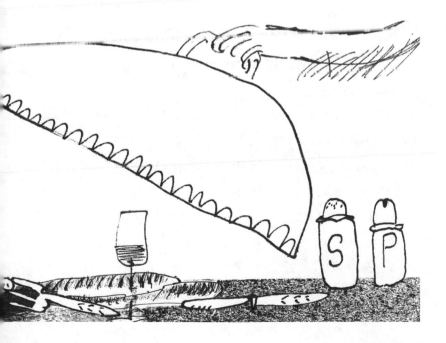

"You've seen that big pile of dirt in their yard. What else is it for?" said Mrs. Priddle. "That's where they *bury* them, Roger. The bones. Think of it—there may be skulls and skeletons and all sorts of other bones." Mr. Priddle was thinking, and he didn't much like the sound of it.

"There's our proof," insisted Mrs. Priddle. "If we take a bag of bones to the police they'll *have* to believe us."

Mr. Priddle lay down again. He had to get up for work in a few hours. "We'll talk about it tomorrow," he murmured. But his wife's hand gripped his shoulder.

"No, Roger, tonight. I can't put up with another night like this. My nerves won't stand it. You have to go tonight."

Fifteen minutes later the Priddles held a council of war in the kitchen. Warren had heard his parents talking and came downstairs to find out why everyone was up. When he heard about the raid next door, he begged to be allowed to take part. If his dad was going to creep around someone's yard in the dead of night, he wanted to be there—especially if there was the chance of digging up some human bones. Mr. Priddle made a show of protesting, but secretly he was glad of the company. The thought of sneaking into the trolls' yard in the dark terrified him.

He was wearing his best black sweater and his face was smeared with dirt. Leaves and twigs stuck out of his floppy gardening hat. He had once seen a film where tough commandos dressed this way so that the enemy wouldn't spot them in the dark (though he didn't remember them wearing gardening hats). Warren's face was covered by the navy ski mask his grandma had knitted him for Christmas. Both of them were armed with flashlights and spades.

"Right," said Mr. Priddle, trying to sound brave and determined. He glanced at the clock: 4 a.m. Soon it would be getting light. He wondered if he would live to see the dawn.

The first problem was climbing over the fence without making a racket. Warren stood on his dad's back and managed to get a foot on the top before jumping over.

"Are you all right, my lambkin?" whispered Mrs. Priddle.

"Fine," came the reply. "Come on, Dad! Hurry up. It's easy!"

Mr. Priddle tried to haul himself up onto the fence, but found his leg wouldn't reach.

"Give me a leg up, Jackie!" he said.

"No, thank you. You've got dirty shoes on," Mrs. Priddle replied.

"Come on! Do you want me to go or not?"

"All right, but watch out for my robe—it's Chinese silk."

With a lot of pushing and grunting, Mr. Priddle managed to get one foot on top of the fence. Gingerly he brought up his other foot. He tried to stand up, tottered for a moment on the top, and finally fell over, landing on top of something soft.

"OW!" yelped Warren.

"Shhh!" hissed Mr. Priddle.

He hoped that trolls slept soundly. What if one of them came out? He would be savaged by a wild, man-eating troll. All they would find of him one day would be a pile of bones and a gardening hat. Mrs. Priddle peered at him over the fence.

"Go on! Don't just stand there!"

"All right," he whispered. "For heaven's sake, Jackie, keep your voice down."

He shone his flashlight at the huge pile of dirt near the end of the yard. It looked bigger in the dark—like some weird-looking mountain. His hands were trembling. "Stay calm," he told himself. "It's just a pile of dirt, that's all. Dirt and possibly skeletons. Human skulls. Nothing to be scared of."

He took several steps toward the mountain. Then the ground disappeared and he fell down into a deep hole with a startled cry. "Arrrooof!"

Inside the house, Mr. Troll was woken by a loud noise. For a moment he thought he was back in his cave in the mountains, but then he felt the soft mattress beneath him—and remembered where he was. Was it the cry of a wolf or a bear that had woken him, or had he imagined it?

Getting up, he looked out of the back window. He caught sight of a tiny beam of light moving in the darkness.

"What is it, hairling?" asked Mrs. Troll's sleepy voice.

"Goblins," said Mr. Troll, grimly. "There are goblins outside."

It was true that Mr. Troll had never actually met a goblin, but he knew all about them. His grandmother had warned him about goblins when he was a little troggler. Goblins were after your gold. They came in the night with their pointy ears and their sacks over their backs. It made little difference that Mr. Troll didn't have any gold— that wouldn't stop goblins. Well, he would give them a nasty surprise. He would teach them a lesson.

He crept into Ulrik's room and shook him, placing a hand over his mouth to stop him crying out.

"Shh! There's goblins in the garden," he whispered.

Ulrik sat up in bed. "Really? Uggsome! Can I see them?"

"Get dressed quickly," said Mr. Troll. "This is a chance for you to do some real roaring. I want you to roar so loud you scare the bogles out of them."

Outside in the yard, Mr. Priddle had managed to clamber out of the hole with the help of Warren. Now they made their way to the foot of the dirt mountain.

"Where do we dig?" asked Warren.

"I don't know. Anywhere," said Mr. Priddle. "As soon as we find anything, let's get back over that fence."

"You're not scared are you, Dad?" asked Warren. "You're shaking."

"Don't be ridiculous, Warren," snapped Mr. Priddle. He dug his spade into the earth but then froze with terror. Out of the dark, a blood-curdling roar reached his ears.

"GRRAAAARR!"

It was followed by a second, not-quite-as-blood-curdling roar from Ulrik.

"Graaarr!"

Mr. Priddle shone his flashlight over the yard. Two angry trolls had burst from the house and were thundering toward them across the lawn. He could see their massive, black shapes and their sharp, white fangs. Beneath his feet the ground was shaking like an earthquake.

"Dad! What do we do?" yelped Warren.

"Run!" said Mr. Priddle, and to show what he meant he dropped his spade and streaked toward the fence faster than a greyhound.

If it hadn't been for the dark, things might have gone badly for the Priddles. An angry troll defending his cave can be ferocious. He will tromp on his enemy with both feet. He will pick them up by the ears and bounce them around like a rubber ball. But this didn't happen to the Priddles because they switched off their flashlights and no one could see a thing in the dark.

Ulrik roared and Mr. Troll roared.

Warren cried, "Dad! Don't leave me!"

Mr. Priddle remembered that in his panic he'd left his son behind just before he fell into the gigantic, muddy hole for a second time.

Meanwhile, at the foot of the earth hill, Mr. Troll caught hold of someone who gave him a hard kick in the shins.

"Yah! Ulrik, that's me," he said.

"Sorry, Dad, I thought you were a goblins!"

"Over there, they're getting away," pointed Mr. Troll, seeing two shadows running for the fence.

Mr. Priddle had managed to climb out of the

hole and was now clambering over the fence with surprising agility. Warren wasn't so lucky— he wasn't tall enough to pull himself up.

On the other side of the fence, Mr. Priddle found his wife waiting for him anxiously.

"Where's Warren?" she asked.

"Run!" gasped her husband.

"But where's my lambkin?"

"Mom! Help!" came Warren's frightened voice from the other side of the fence.

Mr. Priddle reached over. "Grab my hand!" he ordered.

But as Warren was hauled up by his dad, he felt another pair of hands grab him by the legs.

"I've got one, Dad!" cried Ulrik.

"Where are you?" said Mr. Troll, who had blundered into a wheelbarrow.

"Over here, Dad!"

Mr. Priddle pulled and Ulrik pulled. Warren was the rope in a game of tug-of-war. But something was starting to slip down his legs and he decided it was no time for preserving his dignity.

Ulrik fell back on the grass, clutching a pair of pants.

There was a thump from the other side of the
fence and footsteps hurried away.

"What happened?" said Mr. Troll, arriving at last.

Ulrik showed him the pair of black school
pants. "He left these behind," he said.

Mr. Troll held up the muddy pair of pants and
examined them. "Whew!" he said. "Biggest goblins
I ever heard of."

How to Make Friends

ULRIK woke up. The first thing he remembered was that he had to go to school. School today, school tomorrow and the day after. Yesterday morning he had been so eager to find out what school was like, but now he wished he could just stay at home. He liked his new bedroom, which was cozier now that it had a thick layer of mud and leaves on the floor. His mom had promised to look for some cow pies to make it nice and stinksome. He'd begun a mud painting on the wall over his bed—a picture of him playing "Roar and Seek" with his friends in the forest.

The worst thing about school, Ulrik thought, were the "playtimes," which happened twice a day. Peeples seemed to play differently from trolls and he wasn't sure how to join in.

His mom stuck her head around the door. "Ulrik, time to get up!"

"Uhhh!" groaned Ulrik. "I don't feel very well."

"Don't you, my ugglesome? What's the matter?"

"I think I've got the bellies-ache."

"Oh dear, you poor little troggler," said his mom. "Let me see."

Ulrik pulled up his nightshirt to show his round belly. His mom gave him a playful poke in the ribs.

"Ha ha hee! Don't do that!" he giggled, rolling around.

"You don't seem too bad to me. Hurry up and get dressed, breakfast's ready," said Mrs. Troll.

Ulrik plodded downstairs in his school uniform. His dad was already at the breakfast table. Ulrik noticed he had baked bean juice smeared around his mouth.

"I thought you didn't like it," he said.

"I was hungry," said Mr. Troll. "That was fun last night, eh? You and me chasing goblins."

"Yes," said Ulrik. "Did I do okay?"

"You were uggsome," said his dad. "The roaring still needs work, but it's coming along."

"I've been practicing," said Ulrik. "You were scary, Dad!"

"I was, wasn't I?" beamed Mr. Troll. "Frighted

the bogles out of them. Those goblins won't be coming back to rob us again."

"My hairy, scary old husband," laughed Mrs. Troll, kissing him on the snout.

Ulrik smiled. He was glad to see his parents looking happy again. Chasing robbers around the garden in the dead of night was just what his dad needed to cheer him up.

Ulrik still had the muddy pants their visitor had left behind, though personally he wasn't convinced they belonged to a goblin. Inside the label of the pants he had found the letters "WP" scrawled in red. Ulrik had thought it over and WP didn't sound like the name of a goblin. It sounded more like Warren Priddle. He hadn't told his parents his suspicions. There was always the chance his dad would throw a tantrum and storm next door.

Ulrik ate his baked beans slowly, drinking them cold through the holes in the can. Soon it would be time for school and he wanted to put off the moment as long as possible.

"Dad," he said. "You have lots of friends, don't you?"

"Lots back home," agreed Mr. Troll.

"But where did you get them?" asked Ulrik.

Mr. Troll looked puzzled. It seemed like a strange question. "I didn't really *get* them," he said. "Snorvik and Boglov have been my friends since I was a little troggler."

"But you must have started somewhere. I mean what do you *do* when you want to be friends?"

"Do?" Mr. Troll glanced worriedly at Mrs. Troll. He'd never really thought about it. He cleared his throat. "Well," he said. "Say I run into Snorvik, right?"

"Yes," said Ulrik, paying close attention.

"First of all, I'd give him a great, big huggle. Lift him clean off the ground. Then he'd roar and I'd roar back and he'd roar again, and we'd argue about who roars the loudest. Then we'd go off and look for some goatses to chase."

Mr. Troll sat back in his chair looking pleased with himself. It seemed to him that this perfectly summed up the nature of friendship. But it didn't seem to satisfy Ulrik.

"Oh," he said in a disappointed voice, and got down from the table. "Thanks for breakfast, Mom."

"What the bogles was that about?" asked Mr. Troll, mystified.

"I don't know," said Mrs. Troll. "He does seem a bit quiet."

Later, Ulrik trudged along the road on his way to school. "Maybe today will be better," he thought. He would be careful not to bite Mrs. Melly and not to roar in class. If he was quiet, and tried not to look too big, perhaps the other children wouldn't stare at him as if he was about to gobble them up.

Morning lessons passed without any trouble. When the bell rang for break, Ulrik trooped outside with the others. He leaned against the railings trying to look harmless and friendly. The shrieks and laughter from all corners of the playground only made him feel more alone. Everyone else seemed to have friends to play with. His classmates were playing football, trading cards, jumping rope, and talking in groups, but no one came near him. He wondered if he should run up to one of them and give them a mighty huggle. That's what his dad would have done. But they might scream and think he was trying to hurt them.

One of the teachers, Miss Leach, was patrolling the playground followed by a gaggle of small children.

Some boys ran past him, chasing each other. Ulrik recognized one of them as Warren and called out to him. Warren stopped.

"Oh. What do you want?" he said.

"Have you lost your pants?" Ulrik inquired.

Warren looked uncomfortable. "What? Are you joking?"

"No," said Ulrik. "It's just—weren't you in our garden last night?"

"Don't be stupid. I was in bed!" snorted Warren, turning a deeper shade of red.

"Oh," said Ulrik. Perhaps he'd made a mistake.

The other boys had gathered around him, hands on hips. "What are you playing?" Ulrik asked. "Can I play?"

Danny pointed at Ulrik. "We're not playing with him. He's too ugly."

"And he bites," added Rashid.

"I won't," promised Ulrik. He sucked in his fangs so that he looked toothless.

"Come on, why don't we let him play?" said Warren, unexpectedly.

"Can I?"

"Yeah," said Warren. "It'll be fun." He turned to his friends and gave them a sly wink.

"You can be 'It,' Ulrik," he said.

Ulrik beamed. "Uggsome! What is 'It'?"

"Duh!" said Warren. " 'It' means you've got to chase us."

"And catch us," added Rashid.

"All right. Then what?" asked Ulrik.

"Nothing. Whoever you catch is 'It.' That's the game."

"Oh, okay." It seemed too easy. At home Ulrik and his friends played "Pongo"—a game similar to "Tag," only smellier. But Ulrik didn't explain the rules of Pongo[1]—he did as he was told and counted to ten while Warren and his friends ran off.

"Eight . . . nine . . . ten!" he shouted and hurried after them. Although he was much bigger, the boys were quicker on their feet and dodged him time and again. "Yah! Missed me!" they taunted. Ulrik kept chasing them doggedly, till at last he cornered Warren, who was hiding behind rows of plants.

"Ul-rik!" sang Warren. "Come and get me!"

Ulrik didn't really see the garden in its neat stone border. He just trampled straight across it. Tomatoes, lettuce, and sweet peas were squashed to a pulp beneath his size-20 feet.

"Ulrik! GET OFF THERE!" a voice boomed across the playground.

Ulrik turned to see Miss Leach pointing an angry finger at him.

---

[1] In Pongo, the catcher is blindfolded and has to find the other trolls purely by using his sense of smell. If he catches one he sits on him and shouts, "Pongo, Pongo, you are ongo!" If he walks into a tree and knocks himself out, he loses.

"Oh, Ulrik!" said Warren. "Trampling on the school garden. Now you're really in for it!"

Danny and Rashid smirked as Ulrik was led away by Miss Leach. Once again, Ulrik found himself sitting outside the principal's office. Once again he had to endure a long, serious lecture. Mr. Wiseman said it had taken months to grow the plants in the school garden, but it had only taken him a few seconds to destroy them.

"I'm afraid you must be taught a lesson, Ulrik," he said. "No trip to the farm tomorrow—instead, you will stay behind and work."

Ulrik nodded sadly. He'd been looking forward to the trip to the farm. But now he wasn't allowed to go. So far the only thing he'd learned at school was how to get into trouble.

Bubble Trouble

BACK home, Mrs. Troll was dirtying the house. She had noticed a number of ugly, clean patches in the dining room. It took a lot of effort to drag in mud and leaves from outside. The house lacked the homely stench of their old cave. Mr. Troll had grumbled about it that very morning. "If you think it's so stinkless, bring home some cow pies," she'd told him. So he had gone out to look for a cow-pie store and now she was all alone.

Once she had dirtied the house, she sat down at

the table. There wasn't a lot to do. At home she would have taken a walk down to the Hubblings—the natural pools at the foot of Troll Mountain where warm water bubbled up from under the ground. Mrs. Troll would sit for hours in the bubbling soup with her friends, listening to them grumble about their husbands or the sunny weather. Sometimes they made bubbles of their own.[2]

Mrs. Troll missed chatting with her friends at the Hubblings. She had tried sitting in the bath upstairs but it was no fun talking to yourself. "Maybe I should get out of the house and visit someone," she thought. "But who?" She didn't know anyone in Biddlesden. Once or twice she'd seen the peeples next door staring at her over the fence or from an upstairs window. The skinny, bald one was called Roger, and she'd heard him call his mate "Darling." So far Darling and Roger didn't seem very friendly, but Mrs. Troll was prepared to make allowances. "Peeples are shy," she

---

[2] Trolls call this "a gruffler." It is a troll custom to let loose a gruffler after a meal to show your appreciation.

thought. "Not like trolls." Why not go next door and take Darling a gift to show she wanted to be friends?

She looked around the room for a suitable gift and her eye fell on the small pile of rocks on the table. Trolls collect rocks the way some people collect fridge magnets or china cats. In particular, they are fond of rocks that bear any resemblance to a troll. In the garden Mrs. Troll had found a rock that reminded her of a troll's bottom, which she was very proud of. She was sure Darling would like it.

Clutching her gift, she went next door.

Number 8, Mountain View Street, appeared to be empty, but music was coming from some-where inside. After knocking on the door several times, Mrs. Troll walked around the side of the house and peered through the windows. There was no one in the kitchen or in the small room next to it. But at the next window she could hear the music plainly and pushed her nose up against the glass.

Inside, Mrs. Priddle was taking a bath. After the frightening events of the night before she had gotten up late and filled the bathtub to the top with bubbles. From the living room, she was listening to her favorite "Pan Pipes" CD, which she found relaxing in times of stress. If she shut her eyes she could pretend that everything was normal. There were no dangerous trolls living next door, no bones buried in the garden, and nothing to make her nervous. She sank lower in the bath, so that the bubbles rose up to her chin.

Outside, Mrs. Troll was trying hard to get her attention through the window. She waved the rock in her hand to show that she'd brought a gift, but the rippled glass made it hard to see, especially as it was misted up on the inside. She rapped loudly on the window.

Mrs. Priddle's eyes blinked open and she caught sight of the monstrous shadow of the troll at the window. Its huge, ugly face pressed against the

glass, the snout squished to one side. It was smiling horribly. Mrs. Priddle gave a shrill scream and sunk down out of sight. "Roblobb!" she gurgled, which is how the name "Roger" sounds when you say it underwater. But her husband had gone to work and would not be back until six. Warren was at school. She was all alone in the house and not wearing a stitch. Surely this was some horrible nightmare?

The troll had a weapon in its hand—a rock that it was shaking at her. Maybe it was going to smash the window? Mrs. Priddle thought of trying to reach the phone in the living room, but that meant getting out of the bath and she was too rigid with fear to move. If she just stayed where she was, perhaps her visitor would give up and go away.

The troll was tapping on the window, making muffled sounds that might have been threats. At last, its dark shadow vanished. Mrs. Priddle held her breath, listening to the heavy tread of footsteps on the gravel path outside. A moment later she heard it again at the back of the house, rattling the door. It was trying to get in! A thought turned her blood cold. Sometimes Roger went out in the morning and left the back door unlocked. She had told him about it a thousand times. What if today was one of those days? Mrs. Priddle desperately looked around for some kind of weapon. The only thing she could find was Warren's plastic water pistol lying next to the soap.

There was the click of a door opening, followed by a loud slam. The troll was in the house! Mrs. Priddle lay under her white blanket of bubbles, not daring to move.

"Hello, Darling?" called a voice. "It's me!"

Mrs. Priddle didn't answer. The troll was trying to trick her into thinking it was her husband. But she wasn't that stupid. Roger didn't have a deep, growly voice and his footsteps didn't sound like a giant doing a war dance.

She could hear the troll moving through the downstairs rooms, searching for her. For a few seconds everything went quiet and she dared to hope it had gone away. Then a large, hairy head popped around the door.

"Ah! There you are!" smiled Mrs. Troll.

Mrs. Priddle stared at her. She pointed the water pistol with two trembling hands.

"Don't come any closer or I'll fire," she said.

Mrs. Troll held out the oddly shaped rock in her hand.

"I brought you this, Darling," she said. "It looks like a bottom. Not your bottom, of course, but still, you could put it somewhere. Where do you want it?"

Mrs. Troll was doing her best to be chatty, but her neighbor didn't respond—she just kept pointing the thing in her hand. Perhaps it was a gift and she wanted to trade? It was hard to tell. Mrs. Troll reached out for the water pistol and a jet of water squirted her in the eye.

"Oooh!" said Mrs. Troll. It had made a wet patch down the front of her dress.

"Please . . . ," whimpered Mrs. Priddle. "Please!"

"What is it, Darling?" asked Mrs. Troll. It was clear to her Mrs. Priddle wanted something, but she seemed too shy to ask. Steam rose from the bath water and the bubbles looked inviting. Mrs. Troll thought of the Hubblings and how she used to sit and chat with her friends. Perhaps Darling was inviting her to get in?

"Room for a little one?" she said. "You'll have to move over."

Mrs. Priddle didn't realize what was happening until the troll unzipped her dress and started to get into the bath. Then she shot out of the bath like a cork from a bottle.

Pausing only to grab a towel, she ran down the hall and right out the front door. Her screams could be heard four streets away.

"HELP! Murder! Somebody save me!"

Left alone, Mrs. Troll wiped some bubbles from

her snout. She climbed out of the bath with a weary sigh and got dressed. She left the bottom-shaped rock on the television before closing the front door quietly. "Peeples are very strange," she said to herself.

That night, in bed, she told Egbert the whole puzzling story.

"And then the polices came back," she concluded. " 'More complaints,' they said. 'Breaking into peeples' houses. Frighting the neighbors.' "

"Frighting them?" snorted Mr. Troll. "You only took her a rock to be friendly, for uggness sake."

"I know," said Mrs. Troll. "Serves me right for trying to be nice."

"They're as crazy as bees in a bottle," said Mr. Troll. "I asked for some fresh cow pies in a store this morning and they looked at me as if I was talking hogswoggle."

"I know," said Mrs. Troll. "I don't think we'll ever get used to it. We've got no friends, the house doesn't smell right, and every day the polices come around."

"Huh!" grunted Mr. Troll. "At least Ulrik has got friends."

"I hope so," said Mrs. Troll, doubtfully. "He doesn't talk about school much. He's got this farm trip tomorrow, but he hasn't said a word about it." She rested her head on Mr. Troll's shoulder. "Eggy?"

"Mmm?"

"Couldn't we just go home?"

"No," said Mr. Troll, gruffly. "I told you."

"I'm sure the goat thing has blown over. No one wants to make fun of you."

"Oh, no," said Mr. Troll, with heavy sarcasm.

"I'm sure they'll never mention it." He imitated Snorvik's booming voice. "Look, here comes old Egbert. Run into any monster goatses lately, Eggy? Fallen off any bridges?"

Mrs. Troll patted his round belly. "It could have happened to anyone, hairling."

"I can't go back," said Mr. Troll, stubbornly. "We've got to make the best of it here."

Mrs. Troll sighed. Mr. Troll sighed. He got out of the bed and tromped around it a few times, to see if it made him feel better. "Come on," he said at last.

"Where are we going?" asked Mrs. Troll. "It's the middle of the night!"

"Somewhere more comfortable. We'll wake Ulrik."

Twenty minutes later, they were all huddled in the cold, damp subway under High Street.

"It's stinksome," said Ulrik, sniffing the air.

"It is, isn't it?" said Mr. Troll. "Close your eyes and you can imagine you're back in our own buggly old cave."

Ulrik closed his eyes and tried to imagine being home. He imagined the drip, drip of water and the sweet, earthy stench of their cave, the wind moaning outside like an ogre with a toothache.

Above them the city streets were empty, and only the occasional rumble told of a car passing overhead.

Ulrik snuggled between his mom and dad for warmth. Soon it would be daylight and that meant school. He hadn't told his parents that he was banned from going on the school trip. Nor had he mentioned that he'd bitten his teacher and trampled on the school garden. Sooner or later they were bound to find out, and that was the worst part of all.

Big Bad Goat

"**H**E can't stay there on his own," said Mrs. Melly. She glanced through the classroom window where Ulrik was sitting all by himself.

"I told him he was to stay behind," said the principal. "I made it quite clear."

"I know," said Mrs. Melly, "but nobody will have him. I've asked every teacher in the school and none of them wants a troll sitting at the back of the class all day. They say he upsets the other children."

"Then what are we going to do?" he asked.

"Can't he stay with you?" asked Mrs. Melly.

"Be serious! I can't have him in my office; I've got parents coming to see me. What if he bites somebody?"

Mrs. Melly sighed. "Then he'll just have to come on the trip after all. Goodness knows I must be out of my mind. Ulrik on a farm—who knows what he'll do!"

Ulrik wasn't sure why he was allowed on the trip after all, but he was happy to be going. On the bus he sat by himself next to the window, while everyone else sat with friends. Warren was in the back seat with Danny and Rashid. Ulrik could hear them trading potato chips and candy from their lunch boxes. He wished he was sitting with them and had his own lunch box. He began to hum a tromping song to cheer himself up, but he must have hummed too loudly because across the aisle Nisha and Katy Sims were staring at him and snickering.

The farmer peeples who showed them around was named Mrs. Douglas. Ulrik liked her from the start. She showed them the young lambs in their white, woolly coats and the cows being milked in the barn. She let them feed the pigs and climb on the big, red tractor in the corner of the yard. Ulrik asked if he could take a cow pie home but Mrs. Douglas just laughed, as if he had told a very good joke. All the same, he was starting to enjoy himself. Beside the yard he spotted an animal with a black, shaggy coat and two long, curly horns. It was all by itself in a pen.

"A goat!" he said.

"Yes, Ulrik," said Mrs. Douglas. "That's Victor. He's a mountain goat."

"Can we go in and see him?" asked Mrs. Melly.

"No, I'm afraid we keep Victor away from visitors," replied Mrs. Douglas. "He's got a bad temper. Get too close and he might butt you."

Ulrik took a good long look at Victor. He didn't look friendly. Ulrik remembered the giant goat that had tossed his father off the bridge: hooves like iron and horns as sharp as knives. Victor looked like that kind of goat.

Later, Mrs. Douglas left them in the farmyard to eat their lunch, seated on some bales of hay. On the far side of the yard, Warren leaned over the fence watching Victor chew the grass. Suddenly there was a scream of alarm from Katy Sims. The gate of the pen had swung open and Victor had trotted out into the farmyard. Warren was standing by the gate with a mischievous smirk on his face. Victor eyed the children in the yard and gave a low, menacing bleat. "Bahhhh!"

He lowered his horned head and ran at them. Class 4 scattered in all directions, leaving their half-eaten sandwiches behind. Some ran into the gift shop, while others dove into the barn and bolted the door behind them. Ulrik climbed on top of the red tractor, where he found Mrs. Melly looking pale and shaken.

"Mrs. Douglas! The goat got out!" she called.

But there was no answer—Mrs. Douglas was too far away to hear them. Victor trotted around the yard in search of a target. Turning his head, he caught sight of the boy who had opened the gate to set him free. The smirk vanished from Warren's face and the color drained away.

"Warren! Get away from there!" warned Mrs. Melly.

But Warren couldn't move. He was rooted to the spot with fear. The goat was staring at him with its small, mean eyes. It snorted and lowered its horns like a bull that's about to charge.

"Help," croaked Warren in a small, frightened voice.

There was no time to think. Ulrik jumped down from the tractor. He tromped toward the goat, stamping his feet hard to get Victor's attention. When that didn't work, he took a deep breath and bellowed his best roar: "GRARRR!"

It was enough to scatter the sparrows from the trees, but it didn't scare Victor. The goat simply turned its head to see who was making all the noise. It had a black beard wagging from its chin and it looked like it was in an evil mood.

Ulrik tried a second roar but this time it came out as a squeak, like air escaping from a balloon. Faced with a choice of two victims, Victor chose the smaller one and turned his attention back to Warren.

"Stay there, Warren," called Ulrik. "I'm coming."

Ulrik began to inch his way around the yard, keeping close to the fence, until he reached the place where Warren was cornered by the gate.

"Get behind me," Ulrik whispered.

"What are you going to do?" asked Warren.

Ulrik didn't answer. The truth was he didn't know. His plan had been to distract Victor long enough for Warren to escape from the yard, but now the two of them were trapped together. He bravely stepped in front of Warren, blocking Victor's path. The goat tossed its head impatiently, tired of playing games. It kicked up a cloud of dust and lowered its wicked-looking horns. Ulrik knew it was preparing to charge.

"Run, Ulrik!" called Mrs. Melly, peering down from the top of the tractor.

"Run, Ulrik, run!" echoed the voices of Class 4. But Ulrik refused to run. He was a troll and trolls didn't run from goats. His dad hadn't run when he'd faced the giant goat on the bridge. As Victor gathered speed, pounding across the yard toward him, Ulrik did the only thing he could think of. He closed his eyes, opened his mouth, and began to sing.

He sung a song of his homeland, of the blue mountains and the shining lakes.

A few paces short of his target, Victor skidded to an abrupt halt. He cocked his head to one side to listen. He was a mountain goat and this song brought back a long-forgotten memory of the craggy mountains where he grew up. It filled him with such sadness and longing that a tear ran down his long nose and plopped into the dust.

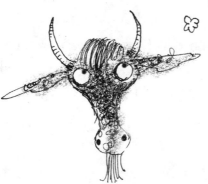

Ulrik opened his eyes, surprised to find that he wasn't flying through the air. When he went closer and stroked Victor's shaggy head, the goat licked his hand and meekly allowed himself to be led back into his pen.

As soon as the gate clicked shut, a big cheer erupted from all around the yard. Ulrik found himself surrounded by his classmates, all talking at once and gazing at him with wide-eyed admiration.

"Ulrik!" said Mrs. Melly, giving him a hug. "That was *so* brave!"

"You were, like, cool!" said Danny.

"You were a hero!" said Nisha, dramatically.

Ulrik was glad that no one could see him blushing beneath his hair.

"Now," said Mrs. Melly. "Where is Warren Priddle?"

Warren came forward looking very small and shamefaced.

"Warren, did you open that gate? The truth, please."

"Yes, Mrs. Melly," mumbled Warren.

"That was a very, very foolish thing to do. If it

wasn't for Ulrik here, someone might have gotten badly hurt. What do you say to him?"

"Thanks, Ulrik," said Warren, sheepishly. He held out his hand. Ulrik opened his mouth to bite it—but just in time, he remembered what had happened last time. Instead he did what trolls do to show they are friends. He lifted Warren right off the ground in a mighty troll huggle.

All Together Now

NINE weeks later, at the end of the school year, there was a concert. The parents sat in rows and listened dewy-eyed to their children singing. Sitting in the front row, taking up four seats between them, were Mr. and Mrs. Troll. They had dressed in their best clothes for the occasion. Mr. Troll sported a red bow tie to match his Bermuda shorts, while Mrs. Troll glittered in a yellow ball gown that she was unfortunately wearing backward. When Ulrik came forward to sing his solo, Mr. Troll couldn't help cheering and stamping his large, hairy feet.

Everyone agreed that Ulrik's singing was the highlight of the concert. In fact, Mr. and Mrs. Troll wept so loudly that they had to be shushed several times. When Ulrik sang, Mr. Troll declared afterward, he could almost smell the pine forests back home.

Afterward, Mr. Troll caught sight of the Priddles and invited them back for dinner, in a burst of generosity. Since the incident with "the crazy goat," the Priddles had softened a little toward their neighbors. Mrs. Priddle no longer screamed when she met one of the trolls on the street. Mr. Priddle no longer spied constantly on his neighbors through his telescope. Even Warren admitted that Ulrik wasn't so bad really—for a troll.

Yet, despite their change of heart, none of them had ever actually set foot inside the trolls' house and they were a little nervous about what they would find.

"Phwar! It stinks!" said Warren as soon they came through the front door.

"Warren!" scolded his mom, but Mrs. Troll seemed flattered.

"I do my best," she said. "I'm afraid the cow pies aren't as fresh as they were."

The Priddles picked their way carefully through the mud and leaves on the floor, worried what they might step in. Luckily, since it was a warm day, Mr. Troll announced they would all sit outside.

An hour later, things seemed to be going fairly well. They had all politely refused second helpings of Mrs. Troll's baked bean and banana pie and were wondering what to talk about next.

Ulrik, who had been waiting for the right moment, appeared from the house with a muddy pair of pants and dropped them in Warren's lap.

Warren recognized them at once and turned pink. "Wh . . . whose are these?" he stammered. "They're not mine!"

"You haven't even looked at them," said Ulrik.

"Give them to me," said Mrs. Priddle, snatching the pants impatiently. "Of course they're yours, Warren! I recognize them. I'd been wondering where these went."

"Mom!" Warren shook his head. "I've never seen them before!"

"Don't be so silly. Here are your initials on the label. WP. I wrote them myself. Wherever did you find them, Ulrik?"

"Well . . . ," began Ulrik, but Mr. Troll interrupted him.

"By the bogles!" he said. "It wasn't goblins in our garden that night, it was you. You were creeping around trying to rob us!"

The Priddles couldn't deny they had been creeping around—the evidence of the pants proved it. They looked at the ground, ashamed and embarrassed. Mr. Priddle took a gulp of Mr. Troll's homemade slug-and-nettle wine, forgetting what was in it. When he'd finished choking he tried to explain.

"We didn't want to rob you, Egbert," he said. "We were just . . ."

". . . Just looking," supplied Mrs. Priddle.

"In the middle of the night?" asked Mr. Troll. "Looking for what exactly?"

Mr. Priddle gulped. "Well, for bones actually," he said. "You see, Jackie somehow got the idea . . . well, that . . . that trolls eat . . ."

"Eat what?" said Mrs. Troll.

"I heard you in the supermarket that day," said Mrs. Priddle. "You asked for a nice, young kid!"

"What's wrong with that?" replied Mrs. Troll. "Goat is Egbert's favorite, and a young kid is nice and tendersome."

The Priddles looked at each other, as their mistake finally dawned on them.

"You mean you were talking about a *goat*?" said Mrs. Priddle. "We thought . . ."

"What?" said Mr. Troll. "That we eat porky little peeples like your Warren?"

The Priddles nodded sheepishly and waited for their neighbors to fly into a rage.

Mr. Troll looked at Mrs. Troll, then at Ulrik. He puffed out his cheeks and exploded with laughter. All three trolls laughed and held their bellies and kicked their legs in the air.

When they had at last recovered, Mr. Priddle said, "I still don't understand. Why dig up all that dirt if it wasn't to bury something?" He pointed at Mr. Troll's gigantic dirt hill, now almost as tall as the house.

Mr. Troll smiled. "What's the name of this road?" he asked.

"Mountain View," replied Mr. Priddle.

"It makes no sense," said Mr. Troll. "There's no mountainses. And no view. Not till now. Come and take a look."

A minute later, the Trolls and the Priddles were all standing on top of Mr. Troll's dirt mountain. Ulrik often climbed up here when he was feeling a little homesick. He could see right across the houses and gardens to a forest in the distance. It was only a molehill compared to Troll Mountain, but it was their own.

"And now," announced Mr. Troll, "we are all going to roar."

"Oh, no, please!" protested Mrs. Priddle.

"Go on, try it," urged Mr. Troll.

"It makes you feel good!" said Ulrik.

"Deep breath," instructed Mr. Troll. "Puff out your chests and roar."

"*GRARRRRR!*"

An earsplitting roar echoed along Mountain View Street and over the neatly cut lawns, so that neighbors looked up and wondered if a jet plane was passing above.

Ulrik smiled to himself. Peeples weren't so bad

once you got to know them, he decided. With a bit more hair you would hardly notice how ugly they were.